P9-CES-714

DEDICATION

For my Aunt Agnes with love and gratitude

And for Princess Lila and Princess Avery,
long may they reign...

AUTHOR ACKNOWLEDGMENTS

The author would like to thank Coco Moffroid
for sharing her extensive knowledge of princesses.

CHOOSE YOUR OWN ADVENTURE®

Kids Love Reading
Choose Your Own Adventure®!

"Thank you for making these books for kids. I bet kids that haven't read it yet would love it. All I can say is that I love your books and I bet other kids would love them too."
Bella Foster, age 8

"These books are really cool. When I get to the end of the page, it makes me want to keep going to find out what is going to happen to me. I get to make my own choices of what I WANT to happen next."
Bionca Samuel, age 10

"This book was good. I like that I got to pick how the story went."
Lily Von Trapp, age 7

"I like how you can make up the story, but it also tells you a story."
Liam Stewart, age 8

"I like to follow the princess and wonder what is going to happen next."
Lilly Boyd, age 7

CHOOSE YOUR OWN ADVENTURE and the CHOOSE YOUR OWN ADVENTURE IN OVAL are trademarks of Chooseco LLC and are registered in the United States and may be registered in jurisdictions internationally. Chooseco's trademarks, service marks, and trade dress may not be used in connection with any product or service that is not affiliated with Chooseco LLC, or in any manner that is likely to cause confusion among customers, or in any manner that disparages or discredits Chooseco LLC.

Princess Island artwork, design and text © 2015 Chooseco LLC
Waitsfield, Vermont. All Rights Reserved.

No part of this publication may be reproduced, stored in a retrieval system, or transmitted in any form or by any other means, electronic, mechanical, photocopying, recording, or otherwise, without the prior written permission of Chooseco, LLC.

Illustrated by Fian Arroyo
Book design by Peter Holm, Sterling Hill Productions
For information regarding permission, write to:

CHOOSECO
P.O. Box 46
Waitsfield, Vermont 05673
www.cyoa.com

A DRAGONLARK BOOK
ISBN-10: 1-937133-50-8
EAN: 978-1-937133-50-4

Published simultaneously in the United States and Canada

Printed in China

11 10 9 8 7 6 5 4 3 2 1

CHOOSE YOUR OWN ADVENTURE®

Princess Island

SHANNON GILLIGAN

A DRAGONLARK BOOK

READ THIS FIRST!!!

WATCH OUT!
THIS BOOK IS DIFFERENT
from every book you've ever read.

Do not read this book from the first page
through to the last page.
Instead, start on page 1 and read until you
come to your first choice. Then turn to the
page shown and see what happens.

When you come to the end of a story,
you can go back and start again.
Every choice leads to a new adventure.

Good luck!

You are a princess, really and truly.

Your official name is:

Princess Peregrine Yvette.

Almost everyone calls you Perri—everyone except your big brother Prince Harold.

"Ready for six weeks away at camp, *Princess Dirt?*" he asks, giving you a shove.

You shove him right back. "Of course, *Prince Claptrap*," you reply.

Claptrap is the polite word for poop. You know this because your father, King Edward, uses it all the time. He says, "That Minister is full of claptrap."

"I told you not to call me that," Harold hisses. He grabs your arm and pinches hard.

Turn to page 2.

"Ow!" you cry.

"Harold, stop pinching Peregrine at once! Is the car packed?" It's your mom, Queen Helena. She comes out of the back door of the Chittenden Palace, where you live. She looks into the back of your big black car.

"All of my stuff is packed, Mom!" you say. "Fishing pole: check. Tennis racket: check. Flashlight: check. Bathing suits and bathing cap: check. Shovel for digging: check."

"Shovel?" Harold sneers. "Why do you need a shovel? They're sending you to camp to learn how to be a better princess. Not a gardener."

"Harold, that's enough," your mother says. "Where's your fencing gear?"

Go on to the next page.

Harold is right. You are *not* very good at being a princess, but you are good at lots of other things. You're good at fixing stuff and making up stories. You like to cook, but you do not like embroidery, or flower arranging, or making chitchat and wearing ball gowns.

The back door slams and you look up. It's your father, King Edward. He gives you a big smile.

"Is her Royal Highness Princess Peregrine Yvette ready for Princess Island?" he asks, scooping you up and twirling you around.

You *think* you are ready. You've been waiting for the first day on Princess Island *all year*.

But you are a little nervous too.

What happens if no one likes you? What happens if you're bored? What happens if you get homesick?

"Tell me about camp again, Mom," you say once the car is beyond the palace gates.

Turn to the next page.

"Well, it's where I went when I was your age. I made some of my best friends there. There are lots of activities. Things like archery and riding, swimming and theater and boating. You get to do whatever you want. But you don't want to do too much of one thing. At the end of the summer, there are the Princess Playoffs," she explains.

"What happens then?" you ask.

"A group of judges mark you on your skills and talents. Your merits and demerits also count. You earn merit points all summer from the counselors and staff for nice things you say or do. Demerits are given when you break the rules or behave badly," she warns. "You can win the Cabin Cup for the highest scoring cabin. And of course there's Top Princess. That's for the best all-around girl with the highest score."

"Fat chance for that, Princess Dirt," Harold whispers.

You just ignore him.

Turn to page 6.

It only takes an hour to reach the launch dock. This is where you will catch a boat out to Princess Island. You hold your mother's hand and walk to the table where the Head of Camp is checking girls in.

"You must be Princess Peregrine," says the friendly woman behind the table with a big smile. She stands up to shake your hand. "Hello and welcome to Princess Island!"

Turn to page 8.

"Good morning, Mrs. Wiggins!" your mother says. The two women give each other a warm hug. "Perri is so excited to be here."

"Well, we are excited to have her," Mrs. Wiggins replies.

Mrs. Wiggins and your mother chat. Mrs. Wiggins checks your name off a list on her clipboard and rifles through a box for your Welcome Packet. You look down at the long cement dock with two large inflatable boats. They are both nearly full with other campers and their gear. You look out across the water to Princess Island, about a mile away.

Go on to the next page.

"Perri, can you answer Mrs. Wiggins, please?" your mother asks.

"I'm s-s-sorry," you stammer. "I didn't hear the question."

"Would you like to take the first boat or the second?" she asks. "There is one seat left on each boat."

You look at the two boats. The first one is filled with girls that all seem to know each other. Most of them look like they are your age. The second boat is filled with older girls. You notice only one girl your age, sitting all by herself.

If you decide to take the first boat to Princess Island, turn to page 10.

If you decide to take the second boat with the older campers, turn to page 17.

"I'll take the first boat," you announce.

You give your mother and father a big hug and kiss goodbye.

"Be good," your father whispers.

"I will," you promise.

A counselor named Catherine helps you wheel your trunk down the ramp. Another counselor who is driving the boat helps you lift it in.

"This is Princess Peregrine," Catherine tells him.

"Hi, I'm Fred," he says, shaking your hand.

"Call me Perri," you say.

"Okay, Perri. Until you pass the Princess Island swim test, you'll need to wear one of these at all times," he says. Fred hands you a foam life vest. You put it on over your dress and tiara and zip it up.

"Okay," Fred yells to your boat. "Everyone listen up."

Turn to page 12.

"While we are moving, no standing up or walking around the boat," he announces in a booming voice. "Find a seat and stay there."

"Why don't you sit here," Catherine says, pointing to an empty spot on the bow. "Can you campers move a little bit to give Perri more room?"

The three girls sharing a secret give you a cool look, and move two inches. You squeeze in next to them and smile, but they turn away. A girl sitting opposite rolls her eyes at them and grins at you. She's wearing a life jacket, too.

Fred starts the engine and backs the boat away from the dock. Everyone waves goodbye to the shore. You wave to your mom and dad and blow them a kiss. They wave back. Your mom wipes a tear from her eye, and your dad hugs her. Harold gives you a baby wave with one hand and picks his nose with the other. He is so gross.

Go on to the next page.

The boat's engine is loud. It's too loud to try to talk to anyone. You watch the lake rushing past. Then you open your Welcome Pack. You are assigned to a cabin called Starflower.

You try to find your cabin on the map. But you are almost there. Fred pulls the boat up next to a huge dock. Two counselors help tie up.

"Everyone's trunk will be delivered to their cabin during lunch," Fred announces. "Please carry only your day pack off the boat."

Turn to the next page.

The Main Lodge sits on a small rise at the top of a large lawn. There must be one hundred and fifty girls and counselors rushing around. You've never seen so many trunks and bags! Senior counselors stand on the docks calling out names, trying to collect their cabins.

"Duchess Chloe Serena!" someone yells.

"Lady Sarah Margaret Wallace!" another shouts.

"Princess Peregrine Yvette!" a voice booms.

Turn to page 16.

"That's me!" you cry. You scramble off the boat and make your way up the dock to the person who called your name.

"Hi there. I'm your cabin counselor. My name is Nathalie," she says. She makes a perfect curtsy even though she is wearing shorts. You curtsy back. "You like to be called Perri, right?" Nathalie seems really nice.

"Yes, please," you reply.

"Good. Perri it is. You're the last one here. The other three girls in Starflower have already gone down to the cabin. You can come with me now and meet them. Or you might want to take the camp tour. It's a great way to get to know a lot of things fast. The next one is about to leave!"

Nathalie points to a cluster of girls gathered to one side of the lawn. You notice the nice girl who smiled at you on the boat is taking the tour.

If you decide to go straight to Starflower with Nathalie, turn to page 22.

If you decide to take the tour of camp first, turn to page 38.

"I'd like to take the second boat," you say.

"Very good," Mrs. Wiggins says.

"The second boat?" a counselor asks. "Follow me!"

"Bye Mom! Bye Dad!" you say. You give your parents a quick kiss and run down the ramp.

"I'm Lady Isabel Farnsworth," the counselor says. "Call me Izzy."

"I'm Princess Peregrine Yvette. Call me Perri," you reply.

You climb aboard. One of the older campers hands you a life vest. "You have to wear this until the swim test. Even at meals," she says.

Really? Wear a life jacket at meals? Several other campers laugh when she says this. The girl your age glances up at you, then looks away. You sit in the empty spot next to her. You say hi, but she only nods. You wonder if that older camper was teasing.

Turn to the next page.

The counselor piloting the boat moves it expertly away from the dock. You are halfway to Princess Island when one of the older girls yells, "Let's go around the island! We've got two new campers on board! Give them the tour!"

The counselor steering smiles and gives a thumbs up. She swerves sharply to the right and floors the engine. Everyone whoops and hollers. You are pointed toward the northern tip of Princess Island.

This is fun!

You round the northern tip of the island.

"This area is off limits," Izzy Farnsworth shouts over the engine noise. "It's an old burial ground."

You peer into the thick woods but don't see anything.

Turn to page 21.

"And that rock formation is called Witch's Hat," she adds, pointing to a spiky rock sitting in a flat round basin.

You look where she points. Something catches your eye just above. It's a woman wearing a long white dress, walking at the edge of the trees.

The girl next to you jerks her head in the same direction.

"Did you just see a . . ." you start.

". . . a woman in white?" she replies before you can finish.

You look at each other.

"Was it a ghost?" you whisper.

No one else has noticed. And now the woman is gone.

"It looked like a ghost," she answers. "I could see right through her."

If you stand up in the moving boat and yell, "Wait! Stop! We just saw a ghost!" turn to page 27.

If you decide to look into the ghost later, turn to page 30.

"I think I'd like to visit the cabin and meet everyone," you tell Nathalie.

"Follow me," she replies.

"The cabins are named after wildflowers," Nathalie explains as you walk. "There are four girls to a cabin. You are put with campers your own age. Several cabins of you younger girls are assigned to one senior counselor. You also have a junior counselor, or JC. Each JC has only one cabin, so you'll see lots of her."

You follow Nathalie down a wooded path as she veers left. You pass a cabin named Indian Pipe. There is a loud scream from inside the cabin called Trillium. Nathalie hurries toward it.

Turn to page 24.

Indian Pipe
Trillium
Sheep Laurel
Starflower
Trout Lily

Bunchberry
Coltsfoot
Wood Sorrel
Foamflower
Leatherleaf
Pipsissiwa

"What's the problem?" Nathalie asks. She knocks and looks through the screen door. Three girls are sitting in a circle with their JC. A fourth girl is standing with her fists clenched.

"There are no private bathrooms in the cabins!" she shrieks.

"That's right," Nathalie replies calmly. "They're in the bathhouse. We all share."

You peer through the screen and your stomach sinks. The girl raising the fuss is your second cousin, Lady Millicent Smythe!

"There are no windows, just screens!" Millicent screeches. "I'm shocked we have lights!"

Millicent has always had bad manners.

If you decide to step forward and say something to your second cousin, turn to page 28.

If you decide to sneak off to Starflower and pretend you don't know Millicent, turn to page 43.

You stand up in the boat and yell, "WAIT! STOP! WE JUST SAW A GHOOOOOOOOHHHHhhhhsss . . ."

But the boat is moving too fast. You lose your balance and topple backward.

You land in the cold water with a loud SPLASH!!

Turn to page 41.

"Hello Millicent," you say. Everyone turns to look.

"Perri! What are you doing here?" Millicent asks. Her cheeks turn a little pink.

"Same as you—working on my manners," you reply. "I can't believe Aunt Anna didn't warn you about the showers."

"Well, she didn't," Millicent says defensively.

You are about to say, "Well, suck it up, Millicent," but you hear the voice of your nanny, Miss York, in your head. *"Princesses don't say 'suck it up,' dear. Princesses say . . ."*

"Millicent, would you like to join me and take the swim test before lunch?" you ask.

First she pauses. Then she turns bright red. You can tell she's trying not to cry.

Go on to the next page.

"I think . . . I think that's a good idea," Millicent sniffles.

"Why don't you all come?" you say to the rest of the girls. "This way we get our tests out of the way. And we can take off these hot life preservers!"

"Great idea," the girls from Trillium say.

The JC smiles. She looks relieved. Nathalie turns and gives you a big wink.

"Three merit points," she whispers. "You just behaved like a true princess."

The End

No one else on the boat has seen the ghost.

"Who do you think she is?" the girl next to you asks.

"I don't know, but I plan to find out," you reply. "Want to come? I'm Perri, by the way."

"You're going to look for the ghost *yourself*?" she asks.

"I plan to look for the ghost the minute we get there. My nanny Miss York always says: Seize the day! The early bird gets the worm! There's no time like the present!"

"My nanny is always warning me not to take risks," the shy girl replies glumly. "She says the world is a dangerous place."

"You need a new nanny, then," you announce.

This makes the girl laugh.

"What's your name?" you ask.

"I'm Caroline, Princess Regent of Ludmilia," she answers.

"Wow! You already run a country?" you ask.

Turn to page 33.

PRINCESS ISLAND

"No, my Uncle Erasmus is running Ludmilia until I turn eighteen," Caroline answers. "Then it's all work and no play."

"So now's your chance," you say. "There's a map of Princess Island in our Welcome Pack. Let's find the exact spot."

You pull out your map to look. Before long, your boat finishes circling the island and arrives at the main dock. The lawn is filled with campers and counselors busy moving in. A bell gongs three times.

"Campers, that's the signal for lunch in thirty minutes," Izzy Farnsworth hollers. "You have time to find your cabin if you hurry."

"Should we find our cabins or look for the ghost?" Caroline asks.

If you decide to look for the ghost right away, turn to page 34.

If you decide to find your cabin first, and look for the ghost later, turn to page 46.

"Let's look for the ghost now!" you say. "I think it's this way."

You point to the map. There is a path behind the Main Lodge. It should lead to the woods where you saw the ghost.

"I'm ready if you are," Caroline says, and grins.

You set off. It's quiet behind the lodge. There is no one in sight. The only sound is the whir of a fan from the kitchen. The path is right where the map says it should be. It leads into a dark forest. There is a sign next to it. You read it out loud:

ABANDON ALL HOPE, YE WHO ENTER HERE

"I guess that's how they say 'Be Careful' here on Princess Island," Caroline says.

You both laugh.

Suddenly the kitchen door snaps open.

Turn to page 36.

"Does anyone know how activities work?" Pandora asks.

"We can do as much of any activity as we want, when we want," the girl next to you says.

"Right, except for your riding lesson. That's at the same time each day," Pandora replies. "Princess Island likes to emphasize individual camper choice. When you first start an activity, let's say archery, your skill level is assessed. You then decide on what level of skill you want to achieve in that activity. There are three levels: Enthusiast, Experienced, and Expert. Counselors help you create a program to reach your goals. It can take several summers to reach Expert status."

Turn to page 49.

"Shhh," you whisper. You and Caroline duck behind a bush.

Two cooks come out on the back porch and start to talk.

"Did you hear that nonsense from the junior counselor this morning? She said she saw a ghost!" the younger woman says.

"It's not nonsense," the older cook answers. "That ghost has haunted this island for over 100 years."

If you stay hidden to hear what else the cooks say, turn to page 55.

If you decide to sneak down the path before you're caught, turn to page 62.

"I'll take the tour," you tell Nathalie.

"Great," she replies. "See you at lunch in half an hour."

You get in line just as the tour is starting. It is led by a junior counselor named Pandora Barden.

"We are standing outside the Main Lodge," she begins. "The lodge is the nerve center of Princess Island. It's where we eat three meals together each day, where you pick up your mail, and where you can shop in the camp store. It's also where the weekly play is performed on Saturday nights and the weekly film is shown on Sunday nights. Please follow me."

Pandora leads you through the different areas of the Main Lodge and out the north door nearest the beach.

"The first bell rings at 7:15 each morning, and again at 7:25. Breakfast begins at 7:45. Breakfast lasts about forty minutes. Then you have a half hour to return to your cabin to brush your teeth and get ready for your day. Activities start at 9:00 AM."

Turn to page 35.

"Girl overboard!" everyone yells.

The boat slows and makes a sharp U-turn.

"Are you okay?" Izzy shouts.

Someone throws you a rope.

"Yes," you sputter.

"Grab the rope," she orders.

The driver cuts the engine. Izzy and two older girls pull you over to the boat and help you in.

"Rule number one of boating: never stand in a moving boat," Izzy says.

"But I . . . we . . . saw a ghost," you say. You point to the shoreline. "Back there."

"You may have seen the ghost of Princess Island, but I still need to give you three demerits," Izzy says.

Izzy orders the boat straight back so you can get into dry clothes. Word of your adventure spreads. You soon earn the nickname "Ghost Girl." (It's better than "Princess Dirt.") You have a great summer at camp and make lots of friends. But in the Princess Playoffs you lose the Cabin Cup by—you guessed it— three demerits!

The End

"Can I continue to my cabin?" you whisper to Nathalie.

She nods and enters Trillium. The screen door slams behind her. You are on your own.

You continue down the path. The next cabin is named Sheep Laurel. The one after that is Trout Lily. Where is Starflower? You would stop for directions, but all the cabins are empty.

Turn to page 44.

You come to a fork in the path and decide to go left. You hear voices up ahead. Maybe it's Starflower?

But when you come around the bend, you see three junior counselors digging a hole in the ground. You are on the back side of the Arts and Crafts building. There is a fancy red leather box on the ground next to them.

"Hurry up, you slacker," one of them says.

The JC shoveling laughs. The other girl looks over her shoulder.

If you just continue because the map says Starflower is straight ahead, turn to page 58.

If you decide to ask for directions to Starflower, turn to page 72.

"I suppose we should find our cabins first," you tell Caroline. "We can look for the ghost after lunch."

"Good idea," Caroline replies.

Your cabins are right near each other. Caroline is in Trout Lily. You're in a cabin called Starflower. As soon as you drop off your backpacks, the lunch bell rings. You follow all the other campers to the Main Lodge. The dining room is full of noise and excitement. Lots of announcements are made. New girls are required to take their swim test right after lunch.

Everyone has to take a tour of the island. All campers must be completely unpacked by dinner, and tryouts for the play this Saturday night will be held after dessert.

You and Caroline both try out for the play. You are the only first-year campers to get speaking roles. Play rehearsals fill every free minute you have for the rest of the week. You won't have time to look for the ghost until after your performance. You and Caroline hope she is still there!

The End

Pandora leads you down to the beach area where watersports take place. These include swimming, diving, waterskiing, kayaking, sailing, canoeing, windsurfing, and wakeboarding.

"There are overnight canoe trips throughout the summer," she adds, "but they require a competency level of Experienced."

Turn to page 50.

Pandora continues past watersports. Next is the Riding Rink and horse barn. You continue to the Arts and Crafts building which is near the tennis courts. You finally pass the Archery Range before arriving at the Singing Circle.

"This is where we meet sometimes for campfires and singing on special occasions. It's also where Princess Playoff winners are announced," Pandora states.

The girl next to you sighs. Her tiara is crooked. She has stumbled over a stone wall near the Riding Rink and ripped her shorts. "My mother was Top Princess," she whispers. "I'm not even going to try."

Go on to the next page.

"It could take some time to get good at stuff," you say. "But don't give up! I bet you'll find something you're better at than anyone else."

"What's your name?" an adult voice behind you says.

You turn around to see who's being asked. Everyone is looking at you. It's one of the senior counselors. You can tell by her blue and white striped shirt.

"Um, I'm Perri, um, I mean Princess Peregrine Yvette. But everyone calls me Perri," you say.

Turn to the next page.

"Well, Perri, I'm Gracie Gruen, and I'm giving you two merit points: one for kindness, and one for encouragement to another camper."

"Really?" you ask.

"Really," Gracie Gruen replies. "That was very nice of you just then."

The camper with the crooked tiara gives you a smile.

"Nice work, Perri," Pandora adds. "And a nice way to end our tour. Here we are, back at the Main Lodge. Lunch will start in five minutes. It's traditional to sit with your cabin mates at the first lunch. I suggest everyone go find them now. Have a great summer on Princess Island!"

You are certain you will.

The End

You motion Caroline to stay and crouch lower.
Suddenly a twig cracks under your foot.
Oops.
The two cooks' heads snap in your direction.
They've caught you spying on their conversation!

"Who's there?" the older cook cries.

You and Caroline slowly stand up.

"I am Caroline, Princess Regent of Ludmilia,"
Caroline says, making a deep curtsy.

"And I'm Perri. I mean, Princess Peregrine Yvette,"
you add. You try to curtsy but you topple over
instead. "We think we saw a ghost."

The old woman chuckles. "You need to work on
that curtsy, missy, before you spend your spare hours
looking for the ghost," she says.

"Who is she?" you ask. "Do you know? We saw her
just now on our boat trip to the island," you add.

"She was wearing a long white dress," Caroline
adds.

Turn to the next page.

"They say it's the ghost of Lady Violet Grimm," the cook begins. "A hundred years ago, her family spent summers here on the island. When she was twenty, she fell in love with a commoner. They planned to run away and get married. But he never came on the appointed day, and she died of a broken heart. Legend says that Lady Violet's father had the lad locked up in prison. Her ghost walks the shore to this day, waiting for him."

Everyone is quiet, letting the story sink in.

"Some things were stupid back then," you announce. "Today a princess can choose who she wants to marry."

Go on to the next page.

"A princess can also choose to go find her cabin before lunch so she and her friend don't get ten demerits each for being on a part of the island that is strictly off limits," the cook says. "You two girls scoot, and no ghost hunting for at least a month." She gives you a wink.

Turn to page 74.

You decide to leave the JCs alone and continue on. Sure enough, the next cabin down the path is Starflower. No one is there. There's a note on the chalkboard next to the screen door. (Every cabin has one.) It says:

We went to the Main Lodge for lunch!
See you there.
– Sam, Bizzy, and Madeleine

You take a quick peek inside your cabin. Yay! It looks like you got a top bunk. You turn back and hurry to the Main Lodge. When you get there, Nathalie waves. She has saved you a seat. You meet your three cabin mates—Elizabeth (or Bizzy), Madeleine, and Samantha (or Sam)—along with Starflower's JC, Lady Amanda. Everyone is super friendly. Bizzy is describing her plan to win the Cabin Cup when Mrs. Wiggins stands up to speak.

Turn to page 60.

"I'd like to welcome all of you to Princess Island. I hope you all learn many skills, have lots of fun, and make lifelong friends. Before I go further, I have an important announcement. A very precious tiara, belonging to Lady Annabelle Campbell, has gone missing. It was in a bright red leather carrying case, and if anyone has seen it or knows anything about its whereabouts, please let any senior counselor . . ."

"I saw it!" you say, raising your hand.

Suddenly, Mrs. Wiggins, Nathalie, Amanda, and all other 150 campers and counselors are looking straight at you. You turn to Nathalie. "Three junior counselors were burying it in a hole behind the Arts and Crafts building," you tell her. "I saw them when I went to find Starflower."

"Which three JCs?" Nathalie asks. Mrs. Wiggins is walking your way. The whole dining room starts talking at once.

You look around and point to the door.

"Those three JCs sneaking out the back," you say. Several girls nearby gasp.

Turn to page 69.

You motion to Caroline to follow you down the path into the woods. You walk so far that you can't hear the two cooks anymore. The forest is cool and quiet. You follow the path as it winds between huge rocks and trees. You check the map.

"That way," Caroline points.

You nod.

"Wait," you say. "Do you hear that?"

You both stop. It's someone crying.

"It's coming from that grove of ferns," Caroline whispers.

If you decide to investigate the crying, turn to page 65.

If you continue on the path to where you both saw the ghost, turn to page 70.

You tiptoe around the ferns and come to a small clearing.

A young woman wearing a white dress sits on a log, weeping. She looks up.

"Have you seen Mathew?" she asks.

"Mathew?" you reply.

"We were going to be married," she says. "But he hasn't come."

"You were going to get married *here*?" Caroline asks.

The woman looks angry. "No, of course not. Mathew is a commoner. We had to marry in secret." She starts to cry again.

"How long have you waited?" you ask.

"One hundred years," she says sadly. Without thinking, your eyes grow wide, and you start to laugh. One hundred years! That's forever!

Turn to the next page.

The woman's face contorts in anger.

"Are you making fun of me? Do you think it's funny I've had to wait a hundred years?"

"I don't think it's funny," you say. "I think it's nuts!"

Suddenly the young woman stands and grows taller and taller and taller, until her white smoky shape looms over you. Her face twists in fury.

"I'll teach you a lesson, you nasty, little. . . ."

You look at Caroline, who yells, "RUN FOR IT!!!!"

Turn to page 75.

Nathalie stands and darts out of the dining room after the three JCs. Mrs. Wiggins is right behind her. They catch up to the girls on the far side of the big lawn. Everyone else runs to the windows to stare.

"Where did you see the tiara?" they all ask. "Did you catch them in the act? Do you know them?"

"Everyone, please return to your seats," Mrs. Wiggins' assistant, Miss Estes, says. She takes over the announcements. First she explains meal times and general safety rules. Then she goes into details about first aid, the camp shop (open from 3 to 4 PM daily), and how to make an emergency phone call home. She is describing try-outs for the weekly play when someone shouts, "There they go!"

Everyone runs back to the windows to see Mrs. Wiggins and Nathalie marching the three JCs to one of the boats. Two groundskeepers follow in a golf cart carrying their luggage.

"Oh my gosh! Wendy Cabot is getting kicked off Princess Island!" someone shouts.

Turn to page 80.

"It's probably someone who is homesick," you whisper. "I think we should continue on the path."

"Me too," Caroline agrees.

The woods are dark and quiet. You walk until you reach a cliff overlooking Witch's Hat on the shore below. There is no sign of the ghost anywhere. You are sure this is where you saw her. The only thing you find is a fancy white lace handkerchief, embroidered with the initials *V.G.*

The final bell sounds for lunch. Your stomach has been growling. It's time to head back. You and Caroline turn the handkerchief in at the Lost and Found in the front office. By the end of the summer, no one has claimed it. Over seven summers at Princess Island, you go back many times to search. Camp legend says the ghost is a princess with a broken heart, waiting for her fiancé. But you never again see any sign of her.

The End

"Excuse me," you wave. "Hello! Over here."

The three girls' heads jerk around.

One of them whispers, "Stop!" to the girl shoveling.

"Hi," another JC says. She smiles a big friendly smile. "Are you lost?"

"I'm looking for Starflower," you reply. "But I might have passed it."

She looks at her watch. "You not only passed it, you're about to be late for lunch." She murmurs something to the two others. "I'm headed to the dining hall right now. Come on with me. We can find Starflower later."

She walks over to join you.

"I'm Wendy Cabot," she says with a quick curtsy. "It's really nice to meet you. I remember when I was new to Princess Island. That was six summers ago. You're going to love it here . . ."

"Princess Peregrine Yvette," you reply. You (sort of) curtsy back. "Call me Perri."

Wendy asks all about you. She laughs at your jokes and gives you tips to pass your swim test. You feel like you have known her forever.

Turn to page 76.

You and Caroline run around to the front of the lodge and collapse on the lawn, laughing.

"I've never 'nearly' gotten a demerit before," Caroline gasps. "That was fun!"

"Stick with me," you say, "and you'll get lots of them!"

Turn to page 82.

You turn and run back the way you came. The ghost is right behind you, screeching at the top of her lungs. You run past boulders and through the glade of pines. You pass the kitchen and race to the front lawn. You feel the icy breath of the ghost on your neck as you round the last corner. The entire camp is getting in line for lunch. At first everyone looks shocked. When the ghost rounds the corner, they get scared.

One hundred and fifty girls and counselors turn on their heels and follow right behind as you run past. She's one mean ghost!

Six weeks later, neither you nor Caroline win the Princess Playoffs. But you *do* receive a special medal for bravery and for proving that the legend of the ghost of Princess Island is true after all.

The End

Wendy Cabot is very popular. Lots of people come over to say hello when you enter the dining room. And everybody asks who you are and wants to be introduced.

"I see you're Wendy's new pet," one JC whispers. "Lucky you. She's the most popular girl on Princess Island. Stick close to her and you'll be near all the action."

You notice other first year campers look with envy in your direction during lunch. When Mrs. Wiggins announces that a very valuable tiara has gone missing, you hardly hear her.

"It's in a red leather box with a handle," she says. "Please report anything you see to me or your senior counselor."

Wendy gives you a huge smile and winks. You just smile back.

Turn to page 79.

Two days later, the girl with the missing tiara is so upset that she leaves camp for good. You feel sorry for her and wonder if you should have said something when you could.

"Should we have said something?" you ask Wendy when you visit her that night after the singing circle.

"Absolutely not!" Wendy replies. "It was just a prank. Camp is full of pranks. Princess Annabelle Campbell needs to learn to take a joke."

It takes just one week for Wendy to forget who you are. You served your purpose, and now she has no time for you.

By then, all the first year campers have made their friends. You spend a lonely summer on Princess Island, wishing you had told the truth.

The End

"I am not sure that's the worst thing that's ever happened," Miss Estes says quietly. Several campers gasp.

"I agree," Amanda says quietly, so only your cabin can hear.

You and your cabin mates all look at her.

"Wendy's not very nice," she explains, blushing. "Even if her father is a powerful Minister. She's a bully."

Two hours later, Mrs. Wiggins and your counselor Nathalie find you in the middle of your swim test.

"Princess Peregrine, I want to congratulate and thank you," Mrs. Wiggins says.

"What for?" you ask.

"Thank you for your honesty, which allowed the safe return of the tiara," Mrs. Wiggins responds. "And congratulations on fifty merit points for courage. Wendy Cabot terrorized many people into silence. I've had an interesting few hours hearing all about it."

Fifty merit points! If you work hard all summer, you might be the first princess in the history of Princess Island to win the Princess Playoffs your very first year!

The End

In fact, the two of you become the best of friends. You spend seven glorious summers in a row at Princess Island, getting into all sorts of trouble. In all those years, despite many hours looking, you never once see the ghost of Lady Violet Grimm.

Mrs. Jenkins, the cook, says that this might not be an entirely bad thing.

The End

ABOUT THE ILLUSTRATOR

Fian Arroyo, with his creative mind and quick draw, has been creating award-winning illustrations and character designs for his clients, including many Fortune-500 companies, in the advertising, editorial, toy and game, and publishing markets for over 20 years. What began as something to do until he found out what he wanted to be when he grew up, has blossomed into a full-time detour from getting a "real job." He has had the pleasure of working with companies such as *U.S. News & World Report*, ABC Television Network, KFC, Taco Bell, *The Los Angeles Times*, SC Johnson, the United States Postal Service and many more.

Originally from San Juan, Puerto Rico, Fian grew up traveling the world as a U.S. Army brat. He graduated from Texas State University in 1986 with a BFA in Commercial Art then moved to Miami, Florida, where he began his freelance illustration career. In 2009, he relocated from Miami Beach to the breathtaking mountains of Asheville, North Carolina where he lives with his wife and two kids.

ABOUT THE AUTHOR

Shannon Gilligan began writing fiction upon graduation from Williams in 1981. She is the author of 15 children's books that have been translated into more than 20 languages. In 1990 she was evangelized by Apple to produce creative software for the CD-ROM platform, and spent almost a decade developing highly acclaimed story-based computer games. The creativity tool Comic Creator, which she produced with her husband R.A. Montgomery, won many awards and was named Best Software by People Magazine in 1995. Gilligan is currently the Publisher at Chooseco LLC, the publisher of all forms of Choose Your Own Adventure. She lives with her dog Gracie in Warren, Vermont and travels frequently. Gilligan used to be a princess when she was little. Kind of.

Watch for these titles coming up in the

CHOOSE YOUR OWN ADVENTURE®

Dragonlarks® series for Beginning Readers

"In a world where children have so little autonomy, my children found delight as they were given the choice to create their own adventure. . . . Fun! Fun! Fun!"

— cyoa.com

SEARCH FOR THE DRAGON QUEEN
DRAGON DAY
RETURN TO HAUNTED HOUSE
THE LAKE MONSTER MYSTERY
ALWAYS PICKED LAST
YOUR VERY OWN ROBOT
YOUR VERY OWN ROBOT GOES CUCKOO-BANANAS
THE HAUNTED HOUSE
SAND CASTLE
LOST DOG!
GHOST ISLAND
THE OWL TREE
YOUR PURRR-FECT BIRTHDAY
INDIAN TRAIL
CARAVAN
GUS VS. THE ROBOT KING
SPACE PUP
FIRE!
PRINCESS ISLAND

"My seven-year-old son was captivated by the idea that he could have a hand in guiding a story about having his very own robot. The story lines kept my son reading over and over. Well done!!!"

— cyoa.com

Purchase online at www.cyoa.com or ask your local bookseller